Me, Frida

BY

Amy Novesky

ILLUSTRATED BY

David Diaz

ABRAMS BOOKS for YOUNG READERS ❋ NEW YORK

The paintings in this book were done in acrylic,
charcoal, and varnish on primed linen.

Cataloging-in-Publication Data has been
applied for and may be obtained from the
Library of Congress.

ISBN 978-0-8109-8969-6

Text copyright © 2010 Amy Novesky
Illustrations copyright © 2010 David Diaz
Book design by Maria T. Middleton

Printed and bound in China
10 9 8 7 6 5 4 3 2

ABRAMS
THE ART OF BOOKS SINCE 1949
115 West 18th Street
New York, NY 10011
www.abramsbooks.com

To Frida, the city I love, and my *querido*, ND
—A. N.

—D. D.

On the warm cobblestone streets of Coyoacán, everyone knew her name. Frida Kahlo lived in the Blue House with her new husband, the famous artist Diego Rivera. Frida was an artist, too.

The night the telegram arrived inviting Diego to San Francisco, Frida dreamed of a city far from her home in Mexico, and she painted a portrait of herself there.

Then she packed her blue trunk, and she and Diego flew north. Frida had never left Mexico before.

Soon they were standing in the very city she'd painted—Diego, big as an elephant; Frida, a lovely little bird on his arm.

They lived at 716 Montgomery Street, in the artists' quarter. Beneath a leaky glass roof and dangling globes of light, they drank *café con leche* and ate sliced oranges.

Outside, the world was cool and gray. Frida felt very far away from home.

Diego was working on a mural for the city. While he sketched, Frida was restless. She strummed a guitar. She sang Mexican folk songs called *corridos*.

"Quiet, *querida*," cooed Diego. He loved his beloved's singing, but there was work to be done.

Before Diego began painting, he wanted to study his subject. Frida followed him as he explored the city. They climbed up and down its many steep hills. They gazed up at its shiny skyscrapers. Diego thought they were great, like ancient ruins. Frida disagreed.

They explored orchards and oil derricks,
a gold mine, and redwood groves. They stood
beneath the towering trees.

Diego felt empowered by everything he saw.
Frida fell asleep on the way home.

And then, with a team of assistants, Diego went to work painting entire city walls.

Some nights, he didn't come home at all.

Other nights, Mr. and Mrs. Diego Rivera attended parties. The city's elite celebrated Diego. Frida stood quietly at his side. No one even looked at her.

On the long days without Diego, Frida felt lost. She was in a foreign city. She didn't speak much English. And she didn't have many friends.

So Frida started exploring the city on her own. She wandered through narrow street markets. She touched pretty birds in tiny, ornate cages and searched in little shops for silk to make skirts. She admired moon-faced babies.

Frida especially loved Chinatown. It smelled of incense, fish, and fog.

Soon Frida felt bolder and rode on a streetcar.
She took a ferry across the Golden Gate and walked
in the green headlands high above the ocean.

From there, she could see the entire glittering
city and all it held, including Diego. It was small
enough to fit on the wing of a bird.

For once, Frida felt larger than life. *Me, Frida!*
She felt like she could fly.

Frida went back to Montgomery Street and painted.
She knew she was an artist, too. While Diego painted
his monumental murals about town, Frida painted
small portraits at home.

The local press called Frida's portraits "passable,"
or good enough. Good enough was not good enough
for Frida. She wanted to be great.

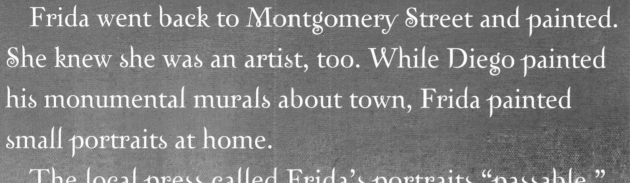

One night, at yet another party, all eyes were on the
great Mexican painter Diego Rivera. Frida stood quietly
at his side. But she could hardly contain herself.
She thought the Americans' faces resembled dough.
She missed Mexico.
And she was tired of being quiet.

Suddenly, Frida began to sing.

Not just any songs, but the Mexican folk songs she sang to Diego while he worked.

All eyes were on her, including Diego's.

"Huzzah!" he shouted at the end of each verse.

He always knew Frida was marvelous.

That night, Frida painted something great: a colorful wedding portrait of herself and Diego. She painted Diego big, and she painted herself small, just as the world saw them.

veis a mi
retratos en
amigo mr

Frieda Kahlo con mi
la bella ciudad de S
Albert Bender   y

But Frida knew she was more than this. And she put herself first. In the beak of a pink bird, she wrote a tiny note on violet ribbon:

"Here you see us, me, Frida Kahlo, with my adored husband Diego Rivera. I painted these portraits in the beautiful city of San Francisco, California . . . in April of 1931."

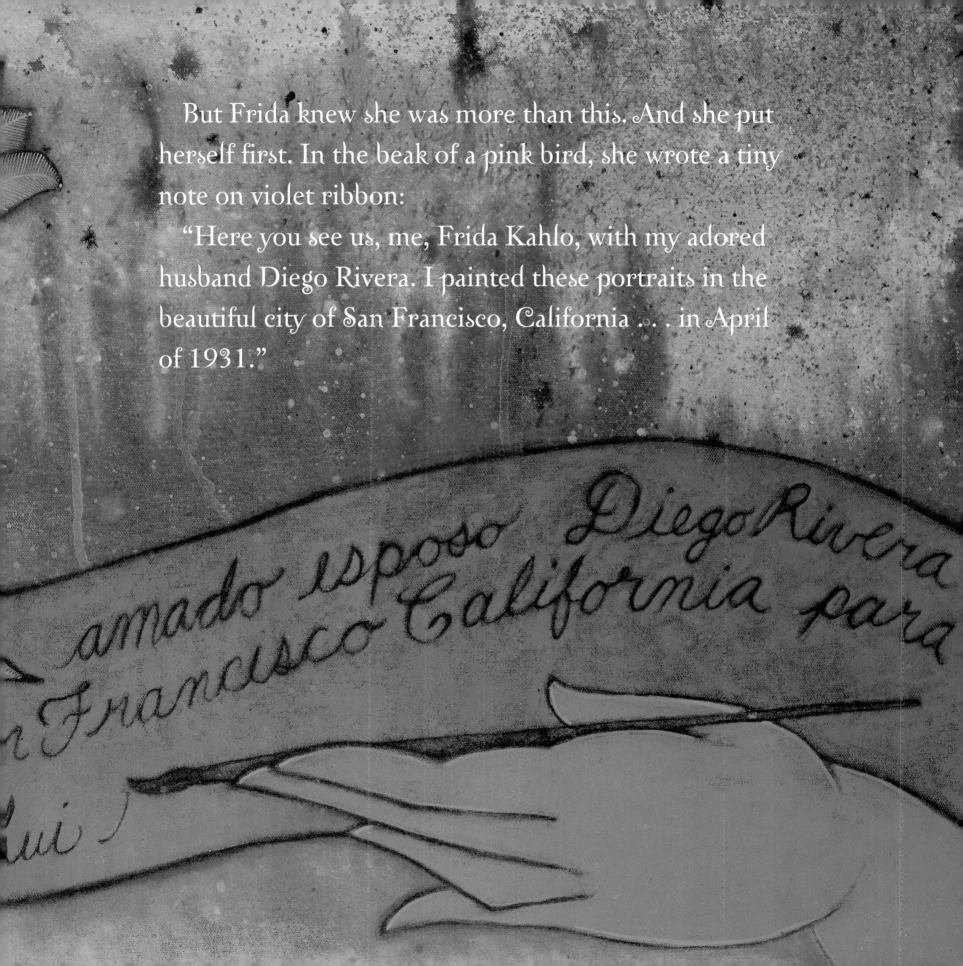

Frida's painting, *Frieda and Diego Rivera*, was featured in the Sixth Annual Exhibition of the San Francisco Society of Women Artists. It was her first show.

Adorned in her best dress and necklaces of ancient jade, her jet-black hair braided, Frida walked proudly through the crowd. When people saw her, they stopped and stared at her in wonder.

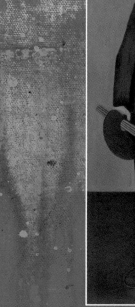

Author's Note

FRIDA KAHLO wasn't a famous artist when she met and married her mentor, the great Mexican painter Diego Rivera. Frida adored Diego. And, to Diego, Frida was tiny and bright, like starlight. She was devilishly brilliant and believed in herself, but she was young and still finding her own unique style.

Frida's move to San Francisco in November 1930 was the first time she traveled out of Mexico. The city of San Francisco inspired Frida and her art. While she was living there, her style moved from broad and mural-like, similar to Diego's, to more intimate and folkloric. Perhaps Frida's distance from her beloved home ignited her pride and her passion for where she came from. *Frieda and Diego Rivera* (Frida sometimes spelled her name "Frieda," in honor of her German heritage) was the first painting Frida created in the style for which she would become famous. It is one of her most-loved paintings.